波波唸翻天系列 4

我愛你，波波！

Justine Korman　著

Lucinda McQueen　繪

本局編輯部　譯

三民書局

For my grumpy valentine with love
—J.K.

把愛獻給我那愛發牢騷的情人
—J.K.

For Jeremy—Your always valentine, Lucy

獻給傑瑞米—你永遠的情人，露西

It was the day before **Valentine's Day**, and Hopper the bunny was even **grumpier** than usual. All his kinderbunny students at Easter Bunny Elementary School were **shrieking** with glee as they made messy **valentines** for their friends and families.

"Who needs candy and flowers and all that **sappy** stuff?" Hopper **grumbled** to himself. "I can't wait until Valentine's Day is over. It's the **corniest** holiday of the year!"

這是情人節的前一天，但是波波卻顯得比平常更不快樂。他在復活節兔寶寶小學裡教的那些學生們，正又說又笑地做著各式各樣的情人卡，準備送給朋友及家人。

「誰會要糖果和鮮花那些笨東西？」波波嘀咕著。「我真希望情人節快點過去。這真是一年裡最無聊的節日了。」

When Hopper was leaving the school that day, **Coach** Cornelius **bounded** up to him. Coach was one of the school's two **gym** teachers. "Hey, Hopper!" he called in a **booming** voice. "Will you help me make a valentine for Marigold? You're **smart** about stuff like that."

那天，當波波正要離開學校的時候，康教練跳上前追上了他。學校裡共有兩位體育老師，他便是其中一位。

「嘿，波波！」他大聲叫。「你能不能幫我做一張情人卡給金花老師呢？我知道你對那種玩意兒最在行了。」

2

Marigold was the other gym teacher at the school.

Hopper hated the whole idea of valentines. But he didn't know how to say no to Coach.

"Oh, all right," the grumpy bunny **sighed**. "What do you want to—"

金花是學校裡的另一位體育老師。

波波實在討厭所有和情人節有關的鬼主意，可是，他又不知道該如何跟教練說不。

「唉，好吧。」這隻愛抱怨的小兔子嘆了口氣。「你想怎麼──」

Just then Hopper heard a voice as sweet as a spring **breeze**. Lilac, the music teacher, was singing as she **hopped** down the school **steps**. She was always singing, **humming**, or laughing. Hopper thought Lilac was the most wonderful bunny in the world.

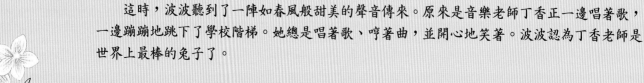

這時，波波聽到了一陣如春風般甜美的聲音傳來。原來是音樂老師丁香正一邊唱著歌，一邊蹦蹦地跳下了學校階梯。她總是唱著歌、哼著曲，並開心地笑著。波波認為丁香老師是世界上最棒的兔子了。

"Good-bye, Coach," said Lilac. "Have a great afternoon, Hopper," she added sweetly.

Hopper wanted to say something, but all he could do was **blush** until Lilac was gone.

「再見了，教練。」丁香說。「祝你有個愉快的下午哦，波波！」她溫柔地加上一句。

波波想開口說話，卻一個字也說不出來，只能滿臉通紅地站在那兒望著丁香，直到看不見她的影子為止。

"So what should I say in my valentine?" Coach asked Hopper.

"Well, let's start with the **basics**," said Hopper. "What do you like about Marigold?"

Coach thought for a second. "She's lots of fun!" he said.

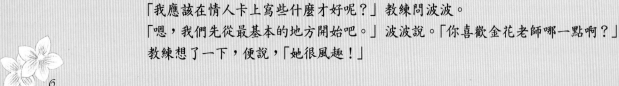

「我應該在情人卡上寫些什麼才好呢？」教練問波波。

「嗯，我們先從最基本的地方開始吧。」波波說。「你喜歡金花老師哪一點啊？」

教練想了一下，便說，「她很風趣！」

Hopper sighed. "Can you be more **specific**?" he asked. "I mean, if I was writing a valentine to, say, Lilac, I would talk about the way she gets everyone to sing, even the **shyest** kinderbunnies, or the way she **tilts** her ears when she's listening, or the way her laugh sounds like music..." Hopper's voice **trailed off** dreamily.

波波嘆了口氣。「你能不能再講清楚一點啊?」他問。「我的意思是說,如果我要寫一張情人卡給,嗯,丁香老師好了,我就會談到她那能使每個人都唱起歌來的本事,即使是那些最害羞的兔寶寶也不例外。還有啊,我喜歡她側耳傾聽的樣子,還有她那像音樂般美妙的笑聲⋯⋯」波波好像在做夢一樣,聲音變得愈來愈小了。

Coach **chuckled**. "Maybe you should write a valentine, too."

"Who, me? Never!" Hopper **scoffed**. "**Besides**, there's no way someone like Lilac would ever want to be my valentine."

教練輕輕地笑著說，「或許你也該寫張情人卡喔。」

「誰呀？我嗎？才不要呢！」波波不屑地說。「而且像丁香老師這樣的好女孩，不可能會願意當我的情人啦！」

8

"You'll never find out if you don't ask her," Coach said. "You know what I always say: Try, try, try—win!"

"Don't coach me, Coach," Hopper grumbled. "Besides, I thought *I* **was supposed to** be helping *you*."

「不問問她，你怎麼會知道呢？」教練說。「你知道的，我常說：試一下，試一下，再試一下──你就會成功的！」

「不用你來教，教練，」波波嘟噥著。「再說，原本我還以為應該是我來幫你才對吧。」

Coach **shrugged**. "OK," he said. "So how do I tell Marigold she's fun?"

"Flowers? Candy?" Hopper **suggested**.

Coach **bounced** his basketball and said, "Marigold doesn't like that stuff any more than I do."

教練聳了聳肩。「好吧，」他說。「那我應該怎麼告訴金花說她是個風趣的人呢？」
「送花好呢？還是糖果好呢？」波波提出建議。
教練拍了拍籃球，然後說，「金花和我一樣，才不會喜歡那些東西呢！」

Hopper **snapped** his fingers. "I've got it! Let's write a valentine on a basketball!"

Coach **grinned**. "You are smart! But what can I say?"

Hopper thought for a minute. "How about this?

*You're my favorite **gal** of all.*
You're more fun than basketball!"

波波彈了一下手指。「啊！有了！我們把籃球當成情人卡吧！」
教練笑開了嘴。「你真是個鬼靈精呢！可是我要在上面寫些什麼才好呢？」
波波想了一會兒。「聽聽看這個如何？所有女孩中我最喜歡妳，妳比籃球還要令我著迷！」

Coach was so happy, he **punched** Hopper on the arm, then gave him a high five.

"That's **perfect**! Thanks, Hopper! You're a real **poet**," Coach said. With that, he jumped out of the house, leaving Hopper a little **confused** and a bit **squished**.

教練高興極了，他用拳頭捶了捶波波的手臂，兩人並且高舉手臂相互擊掌。
「太棒了！謝謝你，波波！你真是大詩人。」教練說。他開心地拍著球，又蹦又跳地離開了屋子，留下有點茫然和不知道該說什麼才好的波波。

A poet — me? Well, maybe I could give it a try, Hopper thought. So he wrote a valentine to Lilac.

我是詩人？嗯，或許我可以試試看喔，波波心裡這麼想著。於是，他寫了一張情人卡給丁香老師。

Hopper was surprised to find that making a valentine was actually fun! He even **trimmed** it with **lace** and added **glitter** and a **bow**.

Now Hopper couldn't wait for Valentine's Day, when he could give Lilac his wonderful card.

波波很驚訝地發現，原來做情人卡竟然這麼有趣！他不但用緞帶在卡片加了花邊，撒上亮晶晶的亮片，並且打了一個蝴蝶結。

現在，波波簡直巴不得情人節趕快來，到時候，他就可以把這張美妙的情人卡送給丁香老師了。

The next morning, Hopper happily **skipped** to school. He ran inside early—and **bumped** right **into** Lilac!

Hopper wanted to give her the valentine. He wanted to say, "Will you be mine?" But **instead** he just stood there, frozen with fear and quiet as a **carrot**.

"Happy Valentine's Day, Hopper!" Lilac sang as she hopped into her classroom.

隔天一早，波波開心地又蹦又跳到學校去。他早早便跑了進去——但卻和丁香老師撞個正著！

波波想把情人卡送給她。他想對她說，「妳願意當我的情人嗎？」可是，他卻只是站在那兒，嚇得一動也不動，像根胡蘿蔔似的一句話也沒說。

「波波，情人節快樂！」丁香老師邊唱邊跳進了她的教室。

I was just surprised to see her, Hopper thought. *I'll give Lilac the valentine at lunch.*

But by lunchtime, Hopper had grown even more **nervous**. In fact, he was so nervous, he **tripped** and dropped his **tray** with a loud ***CRASH!***

我只是太訝異居然會遇到她而已，波波這樣想著。午餐時，我就會把卡片送給丁香老師了。

可是到了午餐時間，波波卻顯得更緊張。事實上，就是因為他太緊張了，結果不小心滑了一跤，整個餐盤匡噹一聲翻倒在地上。

Several schoolbunnies burst out laughing. But Lilac didn't laugh.
She gave Hopper half her sandwich.

　　幾隻兔寶寶忍不住大笑了起來。不過丁香老師不但沒有笑他，還把她另外一半的三明治給了波波。

Hopper was too nervous to eat—and much too nervous to give Lilac the valentine.

"I'm too nervous even to talk!" Hopper said to himself.

波波緊張得吃不下任何東西——也因為太緊張了，遲遲沒把那張情人卡送給丁香老師。
「我緊張得連話都說不出來呢！」波波喃喃自語著。

But then Hopper had a great idea.

I don't have to ask Lilac to be my valentine, he thought. *I'll just **sneak** the card into her classroom and leave it for her!*

He jumped up and hurried out of the lunch room.

但是就在這時候，波波想到了一個好主意。

我根本不必當面問丁香老師是否願意當我的情人，他想。

我只要偷偷地把卡片放在她的教室給她就行了啊！

他馬上跳了起來，匆匆忙忙地蹦出了餐廳。

Luckily, the music room was **empty**. Hopper put the valentine on Lilac's music stand. She was sure to see it there.

Suddenly, Hopper had a thought, and he felt nervous all over again. What if someone else saw the valentine, too? Or what if Lilac thought it was **dumb**? Or what if...

很幸運地，音樂教室裡半個人影也沒有。波波把卡片放在丁香老師的譜架上。放在那邊，她一定會看到的。

突然間，波波想起了一件事，於是又開始不安了起來。如果別人也看到這張卡片該怎麼辦？如果丁香老師覺得這麼做是件很無聊的事，那該怎麼辦？又或者是……

Hopper **grabbed** the valentine and **crumpled** it up. Then he **tossed** it in the **trash**.

"Who am I **kidding**?" he grumbled to himself. "No one would want to be my valentine!"

Hopper was so busy grumbling, he didn't even notice Lilac coming down the hall.

波波抓起了卡片，把它揉成一團，然後扔進了垃圾筒。
「我在開什麼玩笑嘛？」他嘟噥著。「沒有人會想要當我的情人的！」
波波忙著嘟嘟噥噥，沒有注意丁香老師正沿著走廊走了過來。

Hopper was **especially** grumpy the rest of the day.
After school came the worst part of all—the Valentine's Day party.
Hopper looked around at all the pretty **decorations** and happy
schoolbunnies **exchanging** cards and **sharing** pink cupcakes. His
bottom lip trembled a little as he **mumbled**, "Valentine's Day **stinks!**"

接下來的時間，波波感到特別煩躁。

　　放學後，最糟糕的時刻來臨──情人節慶祝會。波波看了看那些漂亮的裝飾，和正在交換卡片，並分享著粉紅小蛋糕的兔寶寶們。他輕輕地動了動下唇，喃喃地說，「令人討厭的情人節！」

Then Lilac stepped up on the stage and sat down at the piano. "I have a special **treat** for you today," she **announced**. "This is an **original** Valentine's Day song written by a very **talented** bunny."

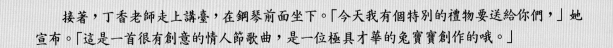

接著，丁香老師走上講臺，在鋼琴前面坐下。「今天我有個特別的禮物要送給你們，」她宣布。「這是一首很有創意的情人節歌曲，是一位極具才華的兔寶寶創作的哦。」

Lilac began to play. "Your voice is sweet like candy treats," she sang. Hopper's ears **perked** up at the very first line. It was his valentine to Lilac! She had set his **poem** to music.

丁香老師開始彈奏，「妳的聲音像糖果一樣甜美，」她唱了起來。

波波一聽到第一句歌詞，耳朵馬上豎了起來。那是他寫給丁香老師的情人節詩句啊！她把他寫的詩譜成了音樂。

Hopper felt himself blushing from head to toe. He also felt as if he would burst with **pride**—especially at the end of the song, when the schoolbunnies **clapped** and Lilac **winked** at him.

波波覺得他全身從頭到腳都羞紅了起來。不過同時也不禁驕傲了起來——尤其是當這首歌結束時，所有的兔寶寶都在拍手，而且丁香老師還向他眨了一下眼睛。

After the **applause**, Hopper walked up to Lilac shyly. "I **guess** you found my card," he said with an **embarrassed** grin.

"Yes," said Lilac sweetly. "It was beautiful."

"I wanted to, um, ask you something," said Hopper. "Would you, um, be my, um, valentine?"

Lilac grinned. "I thought you'd never ask!"

掌聲結束後，波波害羞地走向丁香老師。「我猜妳一定是發現我的卡片了，」他不好意思地笑著說。

「沒錯，」丁香老師甜甜地說。「那張卡片美極了。」

「我想，嗯，問妳一件事。」波波說，「妳願意，嗯，當我的，嗯，情人嗎？」

丁香老師微微一笑。「我還以為你永遠都不會問呢！」

27

As Hopper and Lilac left the school together, they saw Coach and Marigold playing basketball.

"Hi, guys!" called Coach. While his back was turned, Marigold sneaked by him toward the basket.

"Yes!" shouted Marigold, watching the ball **swish** through the **hoop**. "Two points!"

All the bunnies laughed.

波波和丁香老師一起離開學校,他們看到教練和金花老師正在打籃球。
「嗨,你們兩個!」教練打著招呼。他一轉身,金花老師便趁這個空檔轉身上籃了。
「好吧!」金花大喊,看著球咻地一聲進籃。「兩分!」
所有的兔寶寶都笑了起來。

Hopper smiled at Lilac, who smiled back at him. The grumpy bunny had never felt so un-grumpy.

波波向丁香老師微微一笑，丁香老師也對著他微笑。這隻喜歡抱怨的兔寶寶從來沒有感到這麼順心如意過。

"Valentine's Day **turned out** to be pretty wonderful after all," Hopper said to himself that night. In fact, Hopper was so happy that he made up a new **verse** for the Easter Bunny **pledge**:

Who cares if valentines are sappy,
As long as they make someone happy?
And every bunny ought to know
A valentine will help love grow!

「結果，情人節變得如此美好，」那晚波波這樣對自己說。事實上，波波實在太快樂了，所以他為復活節兔寶寶的誓約作了一段詩：只要情人卡能令人歡喜，誰管它是不是肉麻兮兮，每隻兔寶寶都該明瞭，情人卡是愛的催化劑。

announce [əˈnaʊns] 動 宣布

applause [əˈplɔz] 名 鼓掌喝采

basic [ˈbesɪk] 名 基礎

besides [bɪˈsaɪdz] 副 此外，而且

be supposed to 應該……

blush [blʌʃ] 動 臉紅

booming [ˈbumɪŋ] 形 震耳的

bounce [baʊns] 動 使彈起

bound [baʊnd] 動 蹦跳

bow [bo] 名 蝴蝶結

breeze [briz] 名 微風

bump into 和（某人）不期而遇

carrot [ˈkærət] 名 胡蘿蔔

chuckle [ˈtʃʌkl̩] 動 竊笑

clap [klæp] 動 拍手

coach [kotʃ] 名 教練

confuse [kənˈfjuz] 動 困惑

corny [ˈkɔrnɪ] 形 老套的

crash [kræʃ] 名 劇烈的聲響

crumple [ˈkrʌmpl̩] 動 弄皺

decoration [ˌdɛkəˈreʃən] 名 裝飾

dumb [dʌm] 形 愚笨的

embarrassed [ɪmˈbærəst] 動 困窘的

empty [ˈɛmptɪ] 形 空的

especially [əˈspɛʃəlɪ] 副 特別地

exchange [ɪksˈtʃendʒ] 動 交換

gal [gæl] 名 =girl

glitter [ˈglɪtɚ] 名 小亮片

grab [græb] 動 抓

grin [grɪn] 動 露齒而笑

grumble [ˈgrʌmbl̩] 動 抱怨

grumpy [ˈgrʌmpɪ] 形 愛抱怨的

guess [gɛs] 動 猜想

gym [dʒɪm] 名 體育館；體操

hoop [hup] 名 圈，環

hop [hɑp] 動 跳躍

hum [hʌm] 動 哼曲子

instead [ɪnˈstɛd] 副 反而

kid [kɪd] 動 開玩笑

lace [les] 名 花邊

mumble [ˈmʌmbl̩] 動 嘀嘀地說

nervous [ˈnɝvəs] 形 緊張的

original [əˈrɪdʒən̩l̩] 形 有創意的

specific [spɪˋsɪfɪk] 形 明確的

squish [skwɪʃ] 動 使無言以對

step [stɛp] 名 階梯

stink [stɪŋk] 動 令人討厭

suggest [səgˋdʒɛst] 動 建議

swish [swɪʃ] 動 發出咻聲

perfect [ˋpɝfɪkt] 形 完美的

perk [pɝk] 動 豎起（耳朵）

pledge [plɛdʒ] 名 誓約

poem [ˋpo·ɪm] 名 詩

poet [ˋpo·ɪt] 名 詩人

pride [praɪd] 名 自豪

punch [pʌntʃ] 動 捶

talented [ˋtæləntɪd] 形 有才華的

tilt [tɪlt] 動 傾斜

toss [tɔs] 動 扔

trail off 漸漸微弱

trash [træʃ] 名 垃圾（桶）

tray [tre] 名 托盤

treat [trit] 名 款待

trim [trɪm] 動 裝飾

trip [trɪp] 動 絆倒

turn out 演變成

sappy [ˋsæpɪ] 形 愚蠢的

scoff [skɔf] 動 嘲笑

share [ʃɛr] 動 分享

shriek [ʃrik] 動 尖叫

shrug [ʃrʌg] 動 聳肩

shy [ʃaɪ] 形 害羞的

sigh [saɪ] 動 嘆氣

skip [skɪp] 動 跳

smart [smɑrt] 形 聰明的

snap [snæp] 動 彈指

sneak [snik] 動 偷偷放入

valentine [ˋvælənˌtaɪn] 名 情人卡（禮物）

Valentine's Day 情人節

verse [vɝs] 名 韻文

wink [wɪŋk] 動 眨眼

個兒不高・志氣不小・智勇雙全・人人叫好

我是大喜, 別看我個兒小小,

我可是把兇惡的噴火龍耍得團團轉！
連最狡猾的巫婆也大呼受不了呢！
想知道我這些有趣的冒險故事嗎？

探索英文叢書・中高級
Upper Intermediate

中英對照

大喜說故事系列

Anna Fienberg & Barbara Fienberg／著
Kim Gamble／繪　王秋瑩／譯

每本均附CD
（本系列陸續出版中）

精心規劃，內容詳盡
三民英漢辭典系列
學習英文的最佳輔助工具

三民皇冠英漢辭典（革新版）

大學教授、中學老師一致肯定、推薦！
最適合中學生和英語初學者使用的實用辭典！

◎ 明顯標示國中生必學的507個單字和最常犯的錯誤，詳細、淺顯、易懂！
◎ 收錄豐富詞條及例句，幫助您輕鬆閱讀課外讀物！
◎ 詳盡的「參考」及「印象」欄，讓您體會英語的「弦外之音」！
◎ 賞心悅目的雙色印刷及趣味橫生的插圖，讓查閱辭典成為一大享受！

三民新知英漢辭典

一本很生活、很實用的英漢辭典！
讓您在生動、新穎的解說中快樂學習！

◎收錄中學、大專所需詞彙43,000字，總詞目多達60,000項。
◎增列「同義字圖表」，使同義字字義及用法差異在圖解說明下，一目了然。
◎加強重要字彙多義性的「用法指引」，充份掌握主要用法及用例。
◎雙色印刷，編排醒目；插圖生動靈活，加強輔助理解字義。

多種選擇，多種編寫設計
三民英漢辭典系列
最能符合你的需要

三民精解英漢辭典（革新版）

一本真正賞心悅目、趣味橫生的英漢辭典誕生了！
雙色印刷＋漫畫式插圖，保證讓您愛不釋手！

◎收錄詞條25,000字，以中學生、社會人士常用詞彙為主。
◎常用基本字彙以較大字體標示，並搭配豐富的使用範例。
◎以五大句型為基礎，讓您更容易活用動詞型態。
◎豐富的漫畫式插圖，讓您在快樂的氣氛中學習，促進學習效率。
◎以圖框對句法結構、語法加以詳盡解說。

三民新英漢辭典（增訂完美版）

◎收錄詞目增至67,500字（詞條增至46,000項）。
◎新增「搭配」欄，羅列常用詞語間的組合關係，讓您掌握英語的慣用搭
　配，說出道地的英語。
◎詳列原義、引申義，確實掌握字詞釋義，加強英語字彙的活用能力。
◎附有精美插圖千餘幅，輔助詞義理解。
◎附錄包括詳盡的「英文文法總整理」、「發音要領解說」，提升學習效

~ 看的繪本十聽的繪本　童話小天地最能捉住孩子的心 ~

為孩子寫～彩色的夢

 兒童文學叢書

·童話小天地·

- **奇妙的紫貝殼**
  簡 宛·文　朱美靜·圖

- **九重葛笑了**
  陳 冷·文　吳佩蓁·圖

- **銀毛與斑斑**
  李民安·文　廖健宏·圖

- **屋頂上的祕密**
  劉靜娟·文　郝洛玟·圖

- **石頭不見了**
  李民安·文　翱 子·圖

- **奇奇的磁鐵鞋**
  林黛嫚·文　黃子瑄·圖

- **智慧市的糊塗市民**
  劉靜娟·文　邰欣／倪靖·圖

- **丁伶郎**
  潘人木·文
  鄭凱軍／羅小紅·圖

哇～趕快邀進來啊，你爸爸媽媽甜蜜的說故事時間就要開始囉！

國家圖書館出版品預行編目資料

我愛你，波波！ / Justine Korman著;Lucinda McQueen
繪;[三民書局]編輯部譯.－－初版一刷.－－臺北
市；三民，民90
　　面:公分--(探索英文叢書.波波唸翻天系列;4)
中英對照
ISBN 957-14-3443-4　(平裝)

1.英國語言—讀本

805.18　　　　　　　　　　　　　　90003947

網路書店位址　http://www.sanmin.com.tw

©　我愛你，波波！

著作人　Justine Korman
繪　圖　Lucinda McQueen
譯　者　三民書局編輯部
發行人　劉振強
著作財
產權人　三民書局股份有限公司
　　　　臺北市復興北路三八六號
發行所　三民書局股份有限公司
　　　　地址 / 臺北市復興北路三八六號
　　　　電話 / 二五〇〇六六〇〇
　　　　郵撥 / 〇〇〇九九九八——五號
印刷所　三民書局股份有限公司
門市部　復北店 / 臺北市復興北路三八六號
　　　　重南店 / 臺北市重慶南路一段六十一號
初版一刷　中華民國九十年四月
編　號　S 85592
定　價　新臺幣壹佰玖拾元
行政院新聞局登記證局版臺業字第〇二〇〇號

ISBN　957‑14‑3443‑4　（平裝）

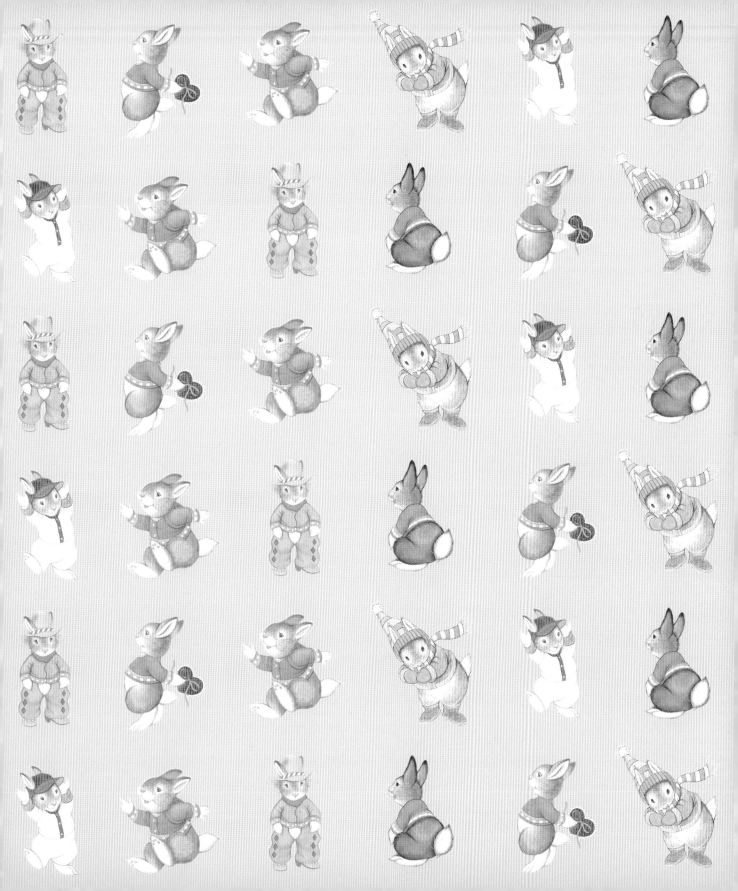